To:

From:

To Jill, Meagan, Linley, and Becky, with love. —GEL

With love for my mom, the best mom a girl could want, and for my girls,
Hannah, Katie, and Megan, the best daughters a mom could wish for. —SLH

For Mya. —SH

Why a Daughter Needs a Mum copyright © 2019 by Gregory E. Lang
Text adapted for picture book by Susanna Leonard Hill
Cover and internal illustrations copyright © 2019 by Sydney Hanson
Cover and internal design by Sourcebooks, Inc.

Sourcebooks and the colophon are registered trademarks of Sourcebooks, Inc.

The art was sketched with pencil and colored pencil, then scanned and painted digitally.

Published by Sourcebooks Jabberwocky, an imprint of Sourcebooks, Inc.
P.O. Box 4410, Naperville, Illinois 60567–4410
(630) 961-3900
Fax: (630) 961-2168
sourcebooks.com

Library of Congress Cataloging-in-Publication Data is on file with the publisher.

Source of Production: 1010 Printing International, North Point, Hong Kong, China
Date of Production: December 2018
Run Number: 5013632
Printed and bound in China.
OGP 10 9 8 7 6 5 4 3 2 1

Why a Daughter Needs a Mum

by Gregory E. Lang   pictures by Sydney Hanson

Adapted for picture book by Susanna Leonard Hill

sourcebooks
jabberwocky

From the first time I held you, so perfect and new,

I promised to do everything that I could do

to help you become your most wonderful YOU,

my darling, my daughter, my girl.

Cheerful, adventurous, loving, and bright,

curious, mischievous, sure that you're right!

I'll help you appreciate your inner light,

and love yourself as I love you.

If someone should say what you value is wrong

or push you aside and say you don't belong,

I'll help you stand up for yourself and be strong

and believe in yourself as I do.

I'll always support you in giving your all

in every endeavor, the big and the small,

and be there to catch you in case you should fall.

I hope you believe this is true.

On days when it seems as though nothing goes right,

just look for the funny side—keep it in sight.

There's nothing like laughter to make your load light!

Chin up! Keep on smiling, my girl.

I'll teach you to notice the world all around.

How mystery, beauty, and wonder abound.

How things to give thanks for can always be found.

Be grateful as I am for you.

I'll listen to you when things weigh on your mind.

We'll talk it all through 'til your troubles unwind.

At moments when life feels a little unkind,

I'll always be right here for you.

We'll try out new styles for our clothes and our hair,

and find the most perfect YOU outfit to wear.

Look your best, feel your best! Then go on out there

and take on the world, my brave girl!

Make sure, my sweet girl, that you find time each day

to **dream**...

to **imagine**...

to **read**…

and to **play**.

Your mind and your heart work much better that way.

My own heart knows this to be true.

I'll teach you to put love in all that you do,

from packing a lunch box to tying a shoe.

Patience makes perfect with anything new.

Love makes the world better, sweet girl.

True friendship's a flower that blossoms with care.

Do what you can to keep arguments rare.

Learn to cooperate, compromise, share,

and hold your friends closely to you.

Sometimes it's hard to be patient, I know.

You want to grow up and your progress is slow.

But the oak started out as an acorn, you know.

You'll get there, my go-getter girl!

Look at the world in your own special way.

Know that a different perspective's okay.

You may not agree with what other folks say.

It's alright to be different, my girl.

Go after the things that most matter to you,

although they may seem quite a challenge to do.

Each day brings you chances to try something new.

Reach for the stars, dearest girl!

I love you for all that you are and will be,

for everything good you have given to me.

You make me the mother I hoped I would be,

my darling, my daughter, my world.